ALICE OSEMAN

HEARTSTOPPER

VOLUME 5

HODDER CHILDREN'S BOOKS

First published in 2023 by Hodder & Stoughton

1 3 5 7 9 10 8 6 4 2

This comic is drawn digitally using a Wacom Intuos Pro tablet directly into Photoshop CC.

A CIP catalogue record for this book
is available from the British Library.

ISBN 978 1 444 95765 5
WTS ISBN 978 1 444 97428 7

Printed and bound in Great Britain by
Clays Ltd, Elcograf S.p.A

The paper and board used in this book
are made from wood from responsible sources.

MIX
Paper | Supporting
responsible forestry
FSC® C104740

Hodder Children's Books
An imprint of
Hachette Children's Group
Part of Hodder & Stoughton Limited
Carmelite House
50 Victoria Embankment
London EC4Y 0DZ

An Hachette UK Company
www.hachette.co.uk

www.hachettechildrens.co.uk

www.aliceoseman.com

CONTENTS

CONTENT WARNING:
Please be aware that this volume of Heartstopper
contains discussions around mental health and eating disorders,
and sexual references. For a more detailed description
of this content, please visit:
aliceoseman.com/content-warnings

And now I have to start thinking about my future plans. I'll be applying to university in the autumn, but I have __NO__ idea what I'm doing with my life.

And I don't know how I feel about moving away from Charlie...

7. TOGETHER

1265

1266

1269

Um... I guess we need to do that at school more often?

Haha ...yeah

1273

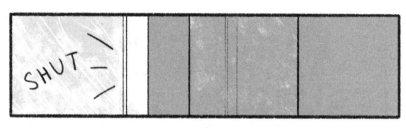

It happened again.

He's talking about sex.

kNOW!!

... It's literally April.

Do you think there's a possibility Nick may have changed his mind since then?

I don't know!

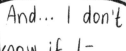

I don't want to pressure him into doing anything.

And... I don't know if I—

?

1279

No.

PULL

Happy Birthday, Charlie!!

Does Tori have a boyfriend?

She won't confirm whether they're actually dating.

1288

Later...

1289

1291

Even later...

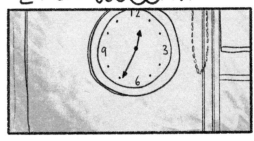

SIP

Come here

TUG

1295

SQUEEZE

1297

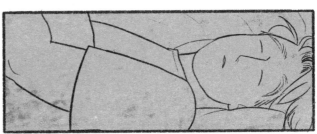

ROLL

MAY

1303

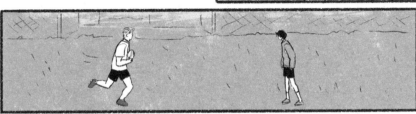

TAC KLE

HA HA HA
HA HA

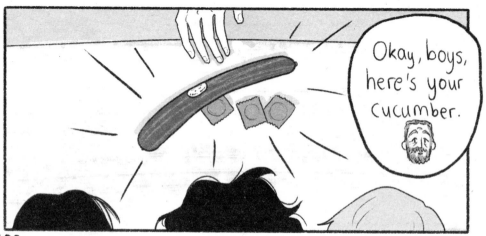

...I take it back.

SIGH

SLUMP

Extra large...?

Charlie—
can you please just ask him if he wants to have sex with you?

FINE.
Okay.
Yes.
I will.

1309

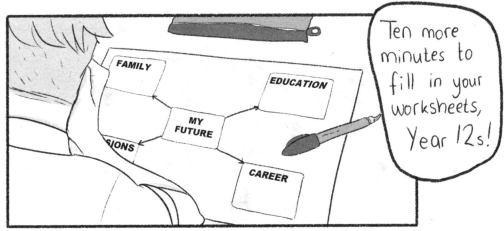

1314

Maybe you should t|

TAP TAP TAP

PAUSE

whoosh

Maybe you should try it not on a cucumber sometime

are you flirting with me or something nicholas

Maybe I am, Charles.......

you are terrible at it

But is it working?

1319

We're now going to look at some examples of STIs.

CLICK

AAAAAAAAAAAH

Look, Charlie, I don't blame you for being nervous about it.

Oh, Charlie! I need to talk to you about the summer fete! Can I message you later?

Yeah, sure!

See you guys at lunch.

1325

FSSSSH

1327

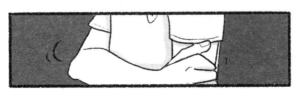

1336

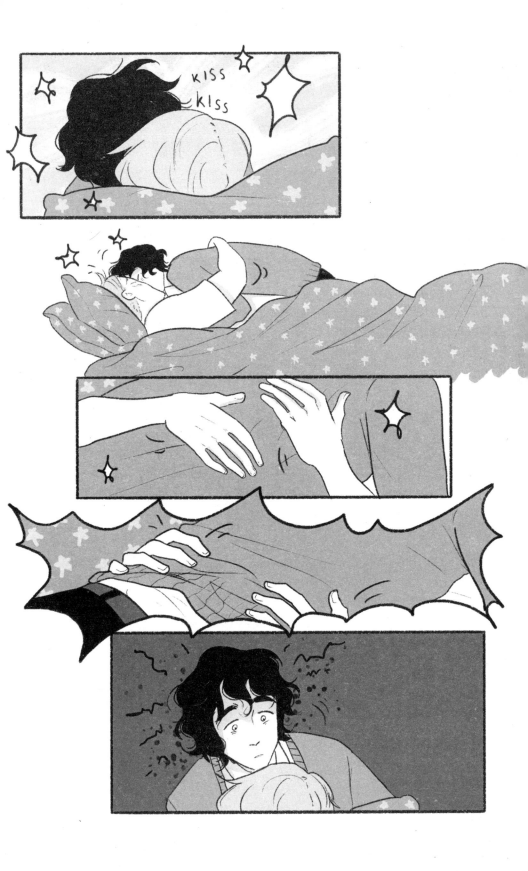

1343

1348

Sahar Zahid

Hey Charlie!! So I needed to ask you a big favour

I'm in a band and we're playing at the summer fete in town in June

I know you play the drums and we really need a drummer

Would you be up for it?

hi!! ooh i don't know, i get nervous about being on stage...

like i've done school orchestra but not an actual proper band

i normally just play by myself haha

Well you can think about it! Let me know!

how many people will be in the audience?

It's an outdoor stage, so... everyone at the fete??

aah yeah wow haha

i'll think about it!! xx

1349

1351

SLUMP

Hey?

Hey

Can I have a hug?

Are you okay?

About what??

What!?

...had a bad dream

You being mean

1353

1355

1357

1362

1363

1365

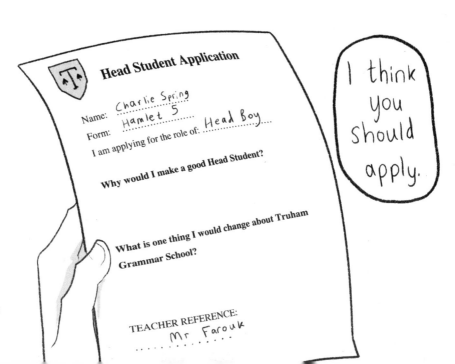

Would I have to, like... do a speech?

There's a speech and an interview in the application process.

...

What is one thing I would change about Truham Grammar School?

I don't know...

I'm not gonna force you.

SHRUG

saturday

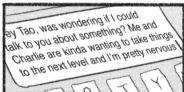

sunday

Hey Tara this is random but

Hey Sai

DELETE

Mum?

Mm?

I was thinking of trying a new recipe for dinner.

Would you help me make it?

1386

Mum?

Mm hm?

Me and Nick were thinking ...maybe I could stay over at his house sometime

PAUSE

Well... yes ...

...at some point.

We were thinking ...soon.

How soon?

I don't know, soon!

...I'm not sure, Charlie.

Why not?

I'm not saying no, it's just—

You've got your GCSE exams and— and this is quite a big step—

And I'm mentally ill so I can't.

No—

No, that's not what I said—

But that's what you're always thinking! You think I'm a baby who can't look after himself!

Why are they upset?

Don't worry, let's go and play Mario Kart

You said... you trusted me.

I— I do, but you're also only sixteen, and you've been very ill—

So I'm not allowed to do anything fun ever!?

I— that's not—

1389

DEEP BREATH

I'm not a child.

And if I want to spend time with my boyfriend,

then I will.

You can't stop me.

Shall we talk about what just happened?

University of Kent I Home | Loughborough Universi | University of Leeds HOME

Type your search here...

PING

19:02

Uni Visits!!!
Tara, Elle, You

Tara Jones
I know we're going specifically to look at unis but I'm soooo excited for our road trip

Elle Argent
Me tooooo

Nick! Let us know if there are any other unis you want to visit on our grand tour!

1398

SHUT

DRRRIIIING

I'm so tired of everyone treading on eggshells around me.

Like, yeah, I'm still working on my anorexia, and some days it's really hard...

but that doesn't mean I can't have fun and do teenage stuff!

1406

1408

1409

When I realised I was bi...

I feel like I woke up.

Because I was repressing so much of myself before then.

Not just my sexuality, but, like, my thoughts and feelings and personality.

It's okay

That didn't make any sense ...

1416

HA HA HA HA

You didn't mind... um...

I kept my shirt on...

1430

SNUGGLE

Does it count as sex?

When it's just touching?

Or is it just, like... third base?

...

I think it counts

Yeah!

1431

1435

SHUT

1439

Don't look at me like that! You come home wearing Michael's clothes all the time!

That's different.

You can just tell me you're dating... It's kind of obvious.

1453

15 MINUTES LATER

UNIVERSITY OF KENT
(day 1)

14:59

But what about when Charlie goes to uni a year later? If he doesn't stay in Kent then you'll still be separated...

Haha yeah... that's true...

Um- I'm gonna go get a coffee

day 2
UNIVERSITY OF OXFORD

1475

Loughborough University

OPEN DAY CHECK-IN ↑

day 3

LOUGHBOROUGH UNIVERSITY

1480

1481

day 4

UNIVERSITY OF LEEDS

1485

1487

1495

day 5

Elle—

No, he needs to hear this!

Nick, you always put everyone else's feelings above your own. And I know you and Charlie love each other, but this is your future.

Like, I know how you feel. I'm in the same boat. But... I have to put myself first right now.

Charlie would support you! He wants you to be happy! Putting yourself first for once wouldn't make him hate you!

It—

It's not just about him.

1500

He thinks I'm putting Kent as my first choice.

Well, you probably shouldn't have said that to him.

ELLE!

No, she's right.

Be honest with him. You're Nick and Charlie. You're gonna be fine.

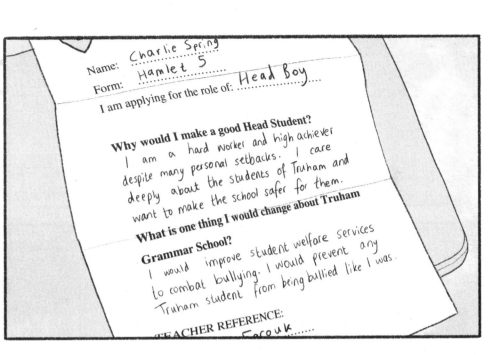

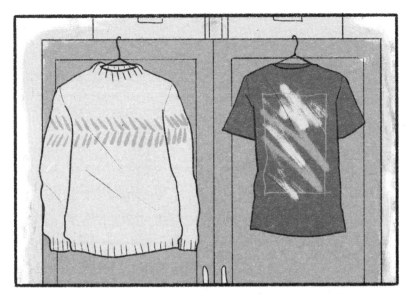

STOMP
STOMP

I wanna go on all the rides and do all the games and win all the prizes

Wow, that's a lot!

Ready to go?

Yup

No Michael today?

Meeting him there.

whoosh

HELTER SKELTER

What does boyfriend and girlfriend mean, anyway? They're just words we've made up to label common experiences within relationships. They shouldn't be important at all. I don't care what society thinks about our relationship as long as we're both happy. If she does ___ ant to label it, I litera___ ___n't care, I just ___ ___igured we should h___ ___ conversati___ about it, ___ but now I wish I hadn't ___ said anything. We don't h___ ___o obey the rules ___ ___f society!

BOP

PING

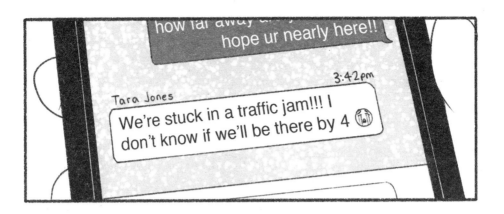

We're gonna miss the band...

PEEK

We've got this!

Next up- a rock band featuring local students from Higgs and Truham Grammar...

VROOOOM

Queer Intentions!

WOO!

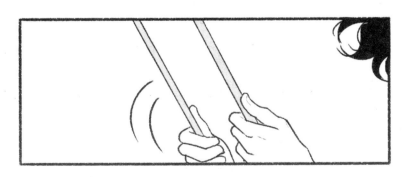

1538

1539

LEAP

1543

1545

You look really good right now

Nick...

Charlie!

You were SO GOOD!

1546

You okay to eat here?

Yeah, I think so... I feel okay today

Hi, can we get two burgers please—

STEP

1559

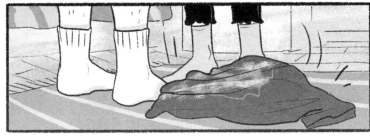

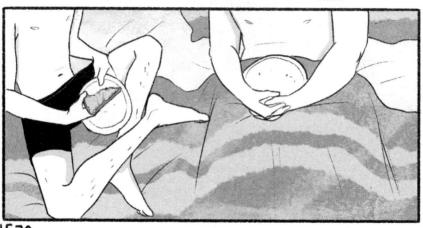

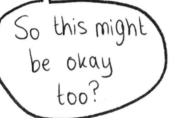

What? Was it bad? Were they all crap?

No, no, they weren't.

Leeds was my favourite.

I think Leeds is gonna be my top choice.

Oh.

It's a really cool campus, like, right in the city, and there's <u>so</u> much to do there, and I got to see one of the rugby teams playing and they seem so cool, and everyone there seems really nice, and I think—

I dunno—

I think I'd really like it there.

1576

Heartstopper will conclude in
Volume 6!

Read the comic online:

heartstoppercomic.tumblr.com
tapas.io/series/heartstopper

CHARLIE SPRING

Nick Nelson

Tao Xu

TORI SPRING

Elle Argent

Tara Jones

Darcy Olsson

Aled Last

Sahar Zahid

Michael Holden

JANE SPRING

JulioSpring

oliver Spring

mr Farouk

Mr Ajayi

Sarah Nelson

Nellie

Henry

Geoff

Sai Verma

Christian McBride

Otis Smith

COACH SINGH

MR LANGE

Aleena

JAY

THE OSEMANVERSE

Year 1

JAN	FEB	MAR
Vol 1 begins		

APR	MAY	JUN
Vol 1 ends Vol 2 begins	Vol 2 ends Vol 3 begins	

JUL	AUG	SEP
Vol 3 ends	Vol 4 begins	

OCT	NOV	DEC
		'This Winter' novella

TIMELINE

Year 2

JAN	FEB	MAR
← 'Solitaire' — 	→	Vol 4 ends 

APR	MAY	JUN
Vol 5 begins		Vol 5 ends

DID YOU KNOW?

Heartstopper doesn't take place in a specific real year

Vol 4 covers the most amount of time ... so far

The 'Nick and Charlie' novella occurs in the summer of Year 3

Author's note

Hello! It's been quite a while! I'm very excited to finally be sharing volume 5 of Heartstopper with you.

Volume 5 took a long time to create because I've spent much of the past few years working on the TV adaptation of Heartstopper. It's been an incredible experience and I feel very lucky to have an adaptation that I'm so proud of and happy with. But without the comic there would be no show, so I couldn't wait to get back to my desk and start drawing again.

We're careening towards the end of Heartstopper now. Last volume, I thought this book would be the end, but it turns out there needs to be one more to complete the story. I'm very sad that the story is ending, but I can't wait to give Nick and Charlie and the Paris Squad the most beautiful send-off in Volume 6.

My heartfelt thanks to my agent Claire Wilson, my editor Rachel Wade, my publicist Emily Thomas, and everyone at Hachette and Heartstopper's international publishers for all your hard work and passion for the series.

Thank you everyone for your love and support for Heartstopper. See you in the final volume.

Alice x

Mental Health Resources

For information, help, support and guidance about mental health and mental illness, please check out the following resources:

Beat Eating Disorders —
www.beateatingdisorders.org.uk

Mind —
www.mind.org.uk

OCD UK —
www.ocduk.org

YoungMinds —
www.youngminds.org.uk

MindOut LGBTQ Mental Health Service —
www.mindout.org.uk

Rethink Mental Illness —
www.rethink.org

Switchboard LGBT+ Helpline —
switchboard.lgbt

Getting it on . . . —
www.gettingiton.org.uk

Collect the whole Heartstopper series!

Read more about Nick and Charlie...

Or read Alice's other prose fiction...

Please go to aliceoseman.com to find out more about the books and their content warnings.